The Cricket
&
The Shepherd Boy

A Christmas Tale

The Cricket and the Shepherd Boy

© Copyright 2010 Reg Down

***

ISBN-10:   1453855033
ISBN-13: 9781453855034

Book Sales:

Lightly Press

lightlypress@gmail.com

This revised edition: 7 January 2013

The Cricket
&
The Shepherd Boy

Written and Illustrated

by

Reg Down

For

Suzanne Down

with whom this story began

as a puppet play for our boys

Aran & Oisin

while

Isa was still flying around in heaven

with angel wings.

Once, a long time ago, there lived a shepherd boy. He had been born with a twisted knee, and because he was lame he walked with a limp and leaned heavily on his shepherd's crook. But he never complained about his leg. He loved being a shepherd and gladly wandered over the meadows and pastures with his flock of sheep.

In summertime he often hobbled to the top of a nearby hill. He looked out over the landscape and gazed at the clouds floating by and tried to guess what shapes they were. Sometimes he saw birds or sheep, and once, in the evening when the clouds were brightly colored, he saw a dragon floating by!

And when he went up the hill early in the morning the meadowlarks rose up from the grass and sang songs of joy to the sun. This he loved best of all!

One day, as he stood on the hill, a cricket chirped in the grass—chirp-chirp, chirp-chirp! He listened, and then stepped closer to hear it better. Instantly the cricket stopped chirping. The boy stood still and waited. Soon the cricket began singing again—chirp-chirp, chirp-chirp! He took another step, but again the cricket stopped.

After a moment he heard a tiny voice: "Don't step on me! Don't step on me!"

"Who's that?" asked the shepherd boy in astonishment.

"It's me! It's me! Can't you see?"

"No, I can't see!" he replied. "Where are you?"

"Here I am! Here I am! Put out your hand."

So he put out his hand and a tiny cricket hopped onto it.

"What's your name?" asked the shepherd boy.

"Chirp-chirp!" replied the cricket. "Chirp-chirp! That's my name— and thank you for not stepping on me."

"You are most welcome," said the boy.

"It's going to be a cold, cold winter," said the cricket.

"How do you know that?" asked the boy. "It's the middle of summer, and very hot. Winter's a long way away."

"I feel it in my knees!" replied the cricket. "I feel it in my knees!"

"Your knees! How can your knees tell you such a thing?"

"Yes, indeed! O yes, indeed! I have special knees," sang the cricket. "This winter's going to be especially cold. And this winter's going to be especially special too!" and with that the cricket hopped off the boy's hand and disappeared into the grass.

"What a funny creature," thought the shepherd boy. "And what strange things to say—even if he does have special knees!"

W inter came, and it was just as the little cricket foretold. It was bitterly cold. The wind blew harshly and heavy snow covered the ground. The shepherd boy had to scrape the snow from the grass to feed his flock, otherwise they would have starved.

E very evening as the sun set he led his sheep to a bluff with an overhanging tree. There they sheltered from the cutting wind and storms.

One night the air was still and calm, but the cold fierce. The moon hung thin and sharp in the night sky and gave poor light. Frost covered the ground and painted the grass and trees. It was so fiercely cold that the frost settled on the backs of his sheep and their fleece sparkled with ice crystals.

The boy and his flock huddled close together for warmth. He was about to fall asleep when he heard a chirping sound: "Chirp-chirp! Chirp-chirp!"

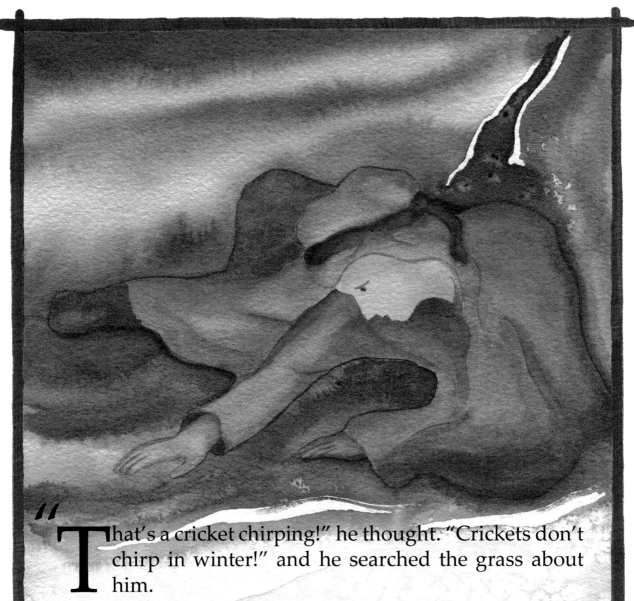

"That's a cricket chirping!" he thought. "Crickets don't chirp in winter!" and he searched the grass about him.

A tiny voice called out: "It's me! It's me! Put out your hand. Put out your hand."

It was too dark to see properly, but he knew at once who it was. So he put out his hand, and quick as a wink the cricket jumped onto his palm.

"What are you doing out and about in the middle of winter?" asked the shepherd boy in amazement. "You should be sleeping deep down in the earth."

"Yes, indeed! Yes, indeed!" chirped the cricket. "You are right! I am right!"

"What do you mean, 'You are right—I am right'?" said the boy. "How can we both be right?"

"Chirp-chirp!" sang the cricket. "Chirp-chirp! You are right that I should be sleeping deep under the earth—and I am right that it is a very cold winter. Am I not right?"

"Yes, you are right," laughed the boy. "But aren't you cold?"

"Oh, yes, indeed! Yes, indeed!" said the cricket. "And if you don't tuck me inside your fleecy jacket my knees will freeze! My knees will freeze!"

Quickly the shepherd boy placed the cricket into his shirt pocket where it was warm and cozy.

"Thank you! Thank you!" chirped the cricket, and began to sing.

"O, this winter is especially cold —
It freeze my nose!
It freeze my toes!
This winter is especially cold,
It freeze my nose and toes!
Hey-ho-the-laddy-O!
It freeze my nose and toes!"

"That's a good song," said the boy. "Sing some more."

So the little cricket sang some more.

"O, this winter is especial-O!
This I know!
This I know!
This winter is especial-O,
It sets my heart aglow-ho-ho!
Hey-ho-the-laddy-O!
It sets my heart aglow!"

"First you're cold and then you're warm!" laughed the boy. "You're not making sense!"

"Oh, yes I am! Yes I am!" replied the cricket. "You'll see! You'll see!" and he continued singing.

"O, this wintertime a Child is born —
He makes me warm!
He makes me warm!
This wintertime a Child is born,
He'll warm me to my knees and toes!
Hey-ho-the-laddy-O!
He'll warm me to my knees and toes!"

"I don't understand," said the shepherd boy. "What child are you talking about?"

"Listen! Listen and you'll find out," chirped the cricket, and sang again.

"O, this winter night a King is come —
Just like the sun!
Just like the sun!
This winter night a King is come,
Born in yonder manger low.
Hey-ho-the-laddy-O!
Born in yonder manger low."

"That's impossible!" exclaimed the shepherd boy. "That manger is only fit for animals!"

"Go see!" replied the cricket. "Go see for yourself."

The shepherd boy was curious. He looked towards the tumbledown shack but could barely see it huddling against a low hill.

W rapping his coat tightly around himself to ward off the chill he set out towards the manger.

As he approached he saw light glowing from inside. Somebody was there! He opened the rickety door and looked in.

There, surrounded by cows and sheep and a little gray donkey, was a father and mother and a new-born child. The father looked old, but wise and kindly, and the mother was as young as springtime.

"Welcome! Come in," greeted the old man.

"Welcome," echoed the young woman quietly. "Come in, young shepherd."

He stepped in and looked around. The manger was warm and filled with light, yet there was no fire and no lantern. All the light and warmth was coming from the child that the mother held.

The shepherd boy was astonished! He had never seen anyone glow with light and warmth just like the sun, and he bowed low to the ground. As he bent over his coat opened and the little cricket hopped out.

"Thank you! Thank you!" chirped the cricket happily. "I knew it! I knew it! I felt it in my knees! I felt it in my knees!" and he started singing as if it were summertime.

The boy went and knelt by the mother. He couldn't take his eyes off the beautiful child. The cricket hopped onto the baby's swaddling blanket and sang so beautifully that the Sun Child fell asleep.

"I think it's time to go," said the shepherd boy at last, putting the cricket back into his pocket. He thanked the mother and the father for letting him see their golden son and left the manger.

Outside, the darkness was lifting.

The shepherd boy climbed his favorite hill and gazed at the rosy light of dawn. What a sight he had seen! But why, he wondered, would the Sun Child be born where no one could know him?

Suddenly the air brightened and an angel appeared. "Greetings!" said the angel. "I bring a message from the highest heavens. There is something you must do."

"Oh, gladly, gladly," replied the boy, falling to his knees. "I will do anything."

"You must tell everyone that the Sun Child, the Light of the World, is born. Go! Tell all who have ears to hear."

"Oh, happily would I do this," said the shepherd boy, "but I am lame and cannot travel far."

"That is your task," replied the angel. "And besides, you are not lame."

The boy looked down, and instead of a twisted knee, he saw that his leg was whole and well. He turned to thank the angel, but she had vanished.

"Praise! Praise!" chirped the cricket. "Now we both have good knees—knees that work just as they should!"

"That's true," agreed the boy, and he let out a shout of joy and leapt high into the air.

"Well! What are we waiting for?" cried the cricket, impatiently hopping up and down in his pocket. "Let's get going! Let's get going!"

So off they went through the world, the cricket and the shepherd boy, singing songs and telling everyone that the Sun Child had been born, that they had seen him with their very own eyes.

The End

More Children's Books by Reg Down

Lavishly and lovingly illustrated by the artist-author,
these books are humorous, sanguine and droll.
They are innocent and magical nature tales, suitable for reading
to young children or for young children to read.

Please visit our website at *www.tiptoes-lightly.net* for updates and upcoming books.
There are also many stories free for downloading for your personal, family, or classroom use.

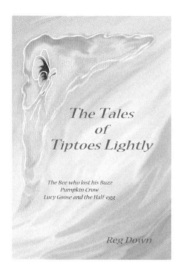

Tiptoes Lightly lives in an acorn high in the branches of a Great Oak Tree. One morning she finds a note lying on her floor. It says: "Please help! Bee has lost his buzz!" She and her friend, Jeremy Mouse, set off down Running River to help the hapless bee. Mr. Cactus, being grumpy, has snagged Bee's buzz on one of his thorns. Thus begins the adventure that takes Tiptoes to the house of Pine Cone and Pepper Pot (they're not at home—just yet), down to the sea to untangle Octopus (he's too young to count his legs properly and gets them mixed up), and up to Snowy Mountain to find out from Jack Frost himself whether he is a gnome (Pepper Pot says he's a gnome because he makes crystals) or a fairy (Tiptoes says he's a fairy because he flies through the air). Jack Frost tells his own creation myth which answers the question in a powerful and striking way.

The Tales of Tiptoes Lightly is comprised of three adventures: *The Bee who lost his Buzz*, *Pumpkin Crow* and *Lucy Goose and the Half-egg*.

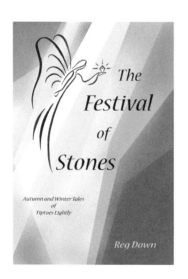

The *Festival of Stones* follows the adventures of Tiptoes Lightly through the festivals of Michaelmas, Halloween, Martinmas, Advent and Christmas. At Michaelmas a real dragon appears, as does St. Michael, and Farmer John tells the story of *The Most Beautiful Dragon in the Whole World* to his children.

Other tales are told too. An angel tells the story of *Martin's Light* at Martinmas; at the Festival of Animals Tiptoes recounts how the animals were sung into the world in *The Myth of Ella-jah*, and Farmer John reads *The Burden Bull of Scotland* to his children on Christmas day. On the way Jeremy Mouse has a frightening encounter at Halloween—with a you-know-what-kind of vegetable!—and almost drowns while sliding on ice (luckily he is saved by Mr. Owl the Vegetarian).

At the farm, the children meet the Borodat who lives in the barn, and on Christmas night June Berry dreams of her mother who has passed over the threshold. In the last chapter the world's first snow-mouse is made by Jeremy Mouse—helped by Tiptoes and the house fairies, Pins and Needles.

Big-Stamp Two-Toes the Barefoot Giant follows Tiptoes Lightly through springtime at Farmer John's. On the way Ompliant the Elephant has his leg pulled by Chit-Chat the Chipmunk, Tiptoes sails down to the sea and brings Spinner the Dolphin back with her to see flowers for the first time, Tom Nutcracker tracks giant footprints into the forest but gets himself treed, and Meadow Mouse almost gets eaten by Tiger the Cat.

Along the way many tales and legends are told: Miranda the spring pixie remembers how the little blue and yellow Forget-me-not was created, a rock spirit reveals how his rock came to be lying in the middle of the forest far away from the mountains (because of Big-Stamp Two-Toes the Barefoot Giant, of course!) and Mr. Rabbit tells the mouselings *The Legend of Oak Knoll Warren.*

Tiptoes' house has no furniture, except for two downy feathers Lucy the Goose gave her to sleep on. Her friends, Pine Cone and Pepper Pot the gnomes, decide to make her a birthday present of one table and three chairs. They search the forest for the perfect branch and enlist the help of forest folk to make the furniture: Ompliant the Elephant to carry the wood, Carpenter Ants to shape the branch and Spinalot the Spider to spin the webbing for the chairs. Unfortunately, Pepper Pot sits down on one of the chairs while the spider web is still fresh and becomes hopelessly flyed. When, at last, he is freed, Pine Cone and Pepper Pot row down Running River to collect wax from the bees to finish the table and chairs. Hauling the table and chairs up Tiptoes' oak tree presents a host of difficulties for the hapless gnomes. Finally, at a surprise birthday party arranged by Jemima Mouse, Tiptoes receives her beautiful presents. Then, at the request of the Mouse children, she tells the tale of how she was born from Mother Wind and Father Sun.

It is spring and Running River is in full flood. Tiptoes Lightly and Jeremy Mouse visit Greenleaf the Sailor and they venture forth in Greenleaf's newly made boat. Soon they are joined by Pine Cone and Pepper Pot the Gnomes and together they search for the Lost Lagoon the frogs have been singing about so beautifully.

Meanwhile, back home, Farmer John reads *The Adam Tales* to Tom Nutcracker and June Berry. Later, Tom rides off in the night until he too comes to the Lost Lagoon. What happens on this night, with its majestic, rising moon, is filled with a wonder and magic that won't soon be forgotten.

One morning an egg appears in the meadow below the Great Oak Tree. Neither Jeremy Mouse nor the fairy Tiptoes Lightly have ever seen such a huge egg – over a foot tall! They go to Farmer John's in search of an answer, but without any luck, and when they return the egg has grown!

Thus begins an adventure which involves most everybody on the farm – human, animal and sprite. The egg, later hidden deep in the forest, keeps growing and finally hatches in a beautiful way on Easter Sunday.

The Starry Bird is an Easter tale with healthy doses of humor, adventure, and just plain fun. But underneath, in a form suitable for children, run the mystery-questions of life, death and resurrection that lie at the heart of Easter.

The Bee who Lost his Buzz is the watercolor illustrated first adventure of *The Tales of Tiptoes Lightly*. It follows Tiptoes Lightly and Jeremy Mouse as they help the Bee whose buzz has been snagged by grumpy Mr. Cactus, the worm who's lost his squirm and cannot wiggle back into the safety of his home, and sail down Running River to the ocean to untangle little Octopus who is too young to count properly (he can only count to seven) and gets his legs hopelessly mixed up whenever he tries.

The Bee who Lost his Buzz is an innocent and magical tale especially suited for reading to young children or for young children to read.

SIR GILLYGAD AND THE GRUESOME EGG

Sir Gillygad is a knight, a doughty knight who rides about on his trusty frog called Gorf. They venture forth on adventures bold and exciting: to the Twinkle, to Holey Hill, to the Plain of Dreams—even as far as World's End. Then rumors were heard, rumors of an egg, a Gruesome Egg, with two leggs, a left leg and a right leg, and the leggs were bird's leggs—which makes sense in an eggy sort of way. It is haunting the Daark Forest close to the Mumbly Mews and the gerwine Greneff. So off Sir Gillygad gallops (well, hoppedy-hops), there to meet and confront this unique and remarkable beast.

Sir Gillygad and the Gruesome Egg is an adventuresome tale, suitable for children aged 9 to 12 or thereabouts—and adults too, if they still are young at heart and open to the wonders that speak to the mystery of life and becoming.

Made in the USA
Coppell, TX
08 December 2019

12575563R00026